FOUR LEGS BAD, TWO LEGS GOOD!

WRITTEN AND ILLUSTRATED BY

D. B. JOHNSON

Houghton Mifflin Company
Boston 2007

FOR
CATRIN AND CLAIRE

The text of this book was handlettered by the artist.
The illustrations are mixed media.

Library of Congress Cataloging-in-Publication Data

Johnson, D. B. (Donald B.), 1944-
Four legs bad, two legs good! / written and illustrated by D. B. Johnson.
p. cm.
Summary: While all of the other animals on a tumbledown farm wait on Farmer
Orvie, a pig, who spends a great deal of time sleeping, an unhappy Duck decides that she
would be a better farmer and sets out to convince Orvie.
ISBN-13: 978-0-618-80909-7 (hardcover)
ISBN-10: 0-618-80909-0 (hardcover)
[1. Leadership—Fiction. 2. Domestic animals—Fiction. 3. Farm life—Fiction.] I. Title.
PZ7.J6316215Fou 2007
[E]—dc22
2006034516

Printed in Singapore
TWP 10 9 8 7 6 5 4 3 2 1

There was a tumbledown farm in Wellingdon where only animals lived.

The shed was leaning on the house.

The house was leaning on the barn.

4 legs bad
2 legs good

NO·MANOR FARM

And
The barn was
leaning on
Farmer Orvie.

He was a pig.

The animals ran from the field to help Orvie.

ORVIE! WE DON'T HAVE TIME TO ROLL DOWN THE HILL!

The animals were not happy.

WE DON'T HAVE TIME TO PLAY IN THE DIRT OR SPLASH IN THE POND!

One day Duck gathered all the animals together.

The animals looked up at the BIG words painted on the barn.

But DUCK was not happy.
She walked around the barn. There was Orvie, snoring in his chair.

Orvie leaned his chair back on its **2** legs.

4 LEGS BAD, **2** LEGS GOOD!

STILL, Duck was not happy.
The next day she woke Orvie from his morning nap.

Orvie pointed at the barn.

I CLIMBED THAT LADDER AND PAINTED THOSE WORDS MYSELF.
YOU CAN'T DO THAT.
A DUCK CAN'T DO ANYTHING REALLY BIG!
4 LeGS BAd
2 LeGS Good
I CAN DO BIG WORK.

That night the animals heard a BIG noise. It was a bubbling, gurgling sound.

It was a chug-a-lug, glug-glug sound.

In the morning the animals ran to see. The pond was empty!

The other animals yelled and ran after DUCK.
They ran faster than Orvie.

They RAN AROUND the house. They RAN through the shed and ACROSS the field. But they COULD NOT catch Duck.

ACROSS the mud hole DUCK flew.

The animals splashed after DUCK.
They RAN RIGHT THROUGH the mud hole.

Orvie followed the animals into the mud. Suddenly he was stopped.

That was when Duck got a rope. She looped it around Orvie.

Duck cheered.

The other animals pulled.

They pulled as hard as they could.

They tugged

and tugged.

And they yanked Orvie right out of his Farmer Boots!

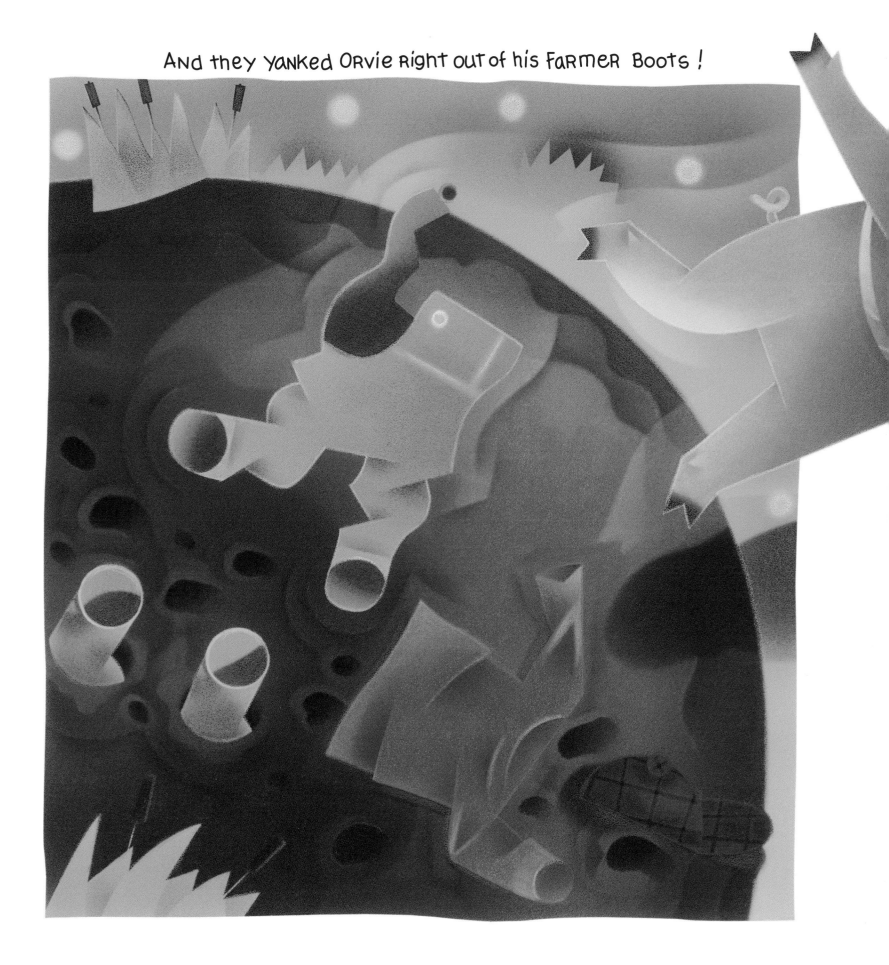

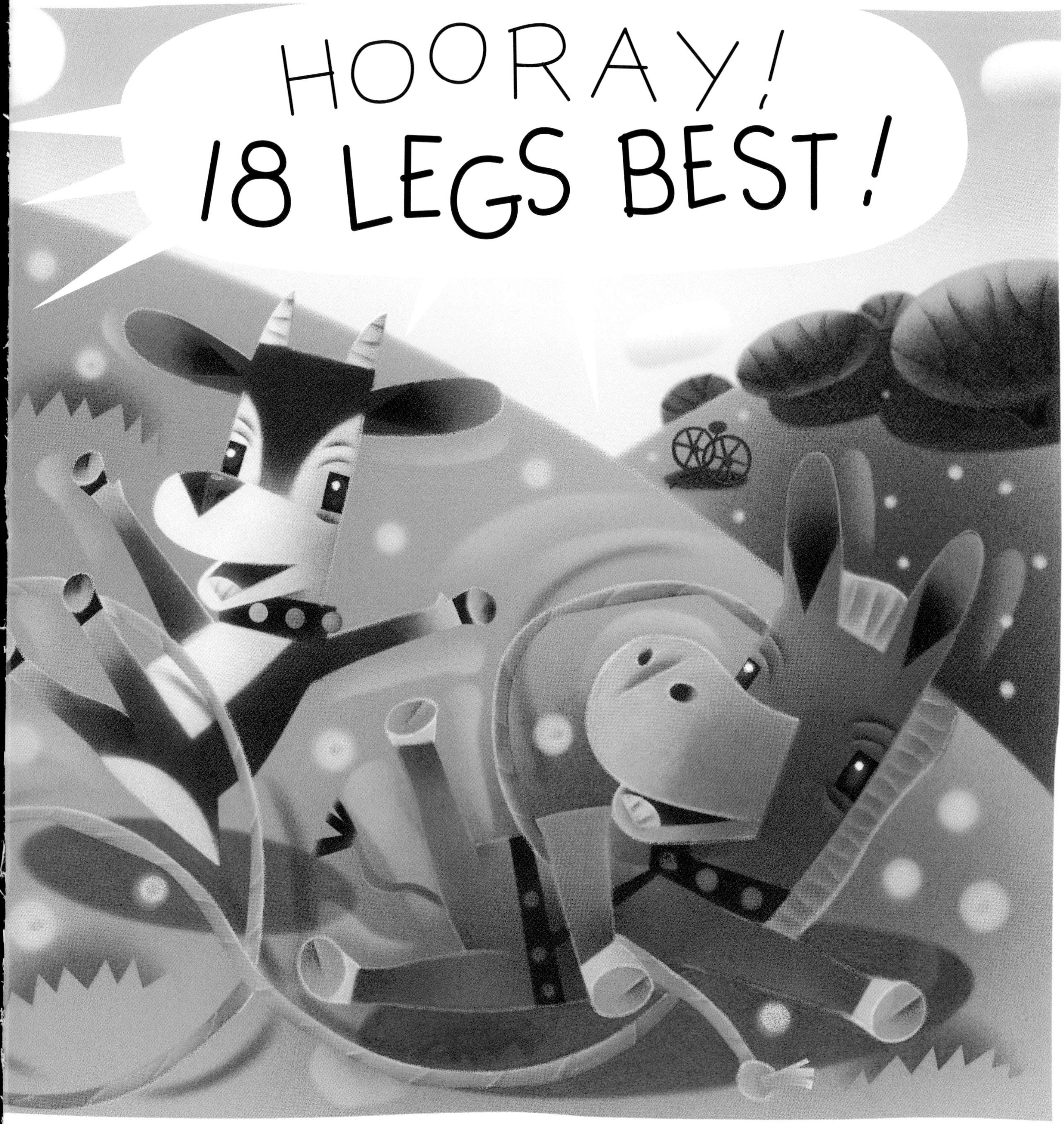
HOORAY!
18 LEGS BEST!

Look what the animals get to do
now that Duck wears the farmer boots!